A treasured gift passed down to Aston, Alvina and children everywhere with love. Cherish them and pass them on to the next generation - F.B.

For Dad and Pam - S.M.

♥

Skip Across the Ocean copyright © Frances Lincoln Limited 1995
Collection copyright © Floella Benjamin 1995
Illustrations copyright © Sheila Moxley 1995

First published in Great Britain in 1995 by
Frances Lincoln Children's Books, 4 Torriano Mews,
Torriano Avenue, London NW5 2RZ
www.franceslincoln.com

Distributed in the USA by Publishers Group West

This paperback edition published in Great Britain in 2007 and the USA in 2008

British Library Cataloguing in Publication Data available on request

ISBN 978-1-84507-788-4

Illustrated with acrylics

Printed in China by Kwong Fat Offset Printing Co. Ltd. in September 2009

9

ACKNOWLEDGEMENTS

Every effort has been made to trace and contact copyright holders before publication. If any errors or omissions have occurred the publisher will be pleased to rectify these at the earliest opportunity.

Lizzie - Ania Chodakowska (Łódź, Poland) and Antonia Lloyd-Jones (London, England); *Wampanoag Lullaby* copyright © Manitonquat 1994; *Schlaf, Kindlein, Schlaf* - Herr Mertens (German Embassy, London, England) and Hanni Zadow (Berlin, Germany); *Lullaby* - Institute of Commonwealth Studies (London, England); *El Coquí* - Joanie Beirne (San Francisco, US); *Cradlesong of the Sparrows* and *Comforting Song* - reprinted with permission of Macmillan Books for Young Children, an imprint of Simon & Schuster Children's Publishing Division, from ON THE ROAD OF STARS, selected by John Bierhorst, Copyright © 1994 by John Bierhorst; *Hush'n Bye* - Joanie Beirne (San Francisco, US); *Èkin, Èkeji, Èketa* - Anthony Adeloye (Nigerian High Commission, London, England); *Canoe Song* - Frankie McKay (Toronto, Canada); *Little White Rabbit* - Scott, THE LAUGHING BABY, reprinted with permission of Greenwood Publishing Group, Inc., Westport, CT. Copyright © Bergin & Garvey, 1988; *Come Harvest* - Yvonne Lundsten (Storuman, Sweden) and Barbro Edwards (Embassy of Sweden, London, England); *Clap Hands* - Veronica Benjamin (Trinidad); *Clap Handies* - Mary Anthony (Kerry, Ireland); *Gee up a Chapallín* - Thomas O'Rourke (Kerry, Ireland) and Gearóid Ó Crualaoich (Béaloideas, UCC, Cork, Ireland); *The Singing Bird* - Reprinted by permission of University of Tennessee Press. "The Singing Bird" from THE COMPLETE PEDDLER'S PACK by May Justus, Copyright © 1967 by the University of Tennessee Press; *Liuli, Liuli, Liuli* Scott, THE LAUGHING BABY, reprinted with permission of Greenwood Publishing Group, Inc., Westport, CT. Copyright © Bergin & Garvey, 1988; *Above the Rooftops* - Caroline Lewis (Japanese Embassy, London, England); *Little Elephant Swaying* - Mrs Patel (London, England); *Kaleeba!* - Margaret Williams (Commonwealth Institute, London, England) and Fred Ssemugera and family (Chairman, Ebika Bya Baganda e Bungereza, London, England); *Lullaby of a Dog to Her Pup* - reprinted with permission of Macmillan Books for Young Children, an imprint of Simon & Schuster Children's Publishing Division, from ON THE ROAD OF STARS, selected by John Bierhorst, Copyright © 1994 by John Bierhorst; *Little Bird* - Scott, THE LAUGHING BABY, reprinted with permission of Greenwood Publishing Group, Inc., Westport, CT. Copyright © Bergin & Garvey, 1988; *Kella Buck* - Greta Høien (Oslo, Norway) and Anne-Karin Stockinger (Royal Norwegian Embassy, London, England); *Eeny Meeny* - Ingrid and John Court-Jones (Torquay, England); *Kye Kye Kule* - Margaret Williams (Commonwealth Institute, London, England) and Clara Hagan (London, England); *Children, Children* - Roy Benjamin (Antigua); *Al Corro de la Patata* - Maria Acuna (Barcelona, Spain) and Jose Maria Jimenez (Madrid, Spain); *Kookaburra* - Marion Sinclair, Copyright © Larrikin Music Publishing Pty Ltd, Campbell Connelly & Co. Ltd, 8/9 Frith Street, London, W1V 5TZ. Used by permission. All rights reserved; *Pulling the Saw* - Scott, THE LAUGHING BABY, reprinted with permission of Greenwood Publishing Group, Inc., Westport, CT. Copyright © Bergin & Garvey, 1988.

WITH GRATEFUL THANKS FOR THEIR HELP:

Abiola Ogunsola, Nandini Mane, Wale Adeagbo, Steph Smith and Lorna Stoddart (The Working Group Against Racism in Children's Resources, London, England) for their advice on the text; Colm and Traolach MacCuinn (Kerry, Ireland); Amanda Dargan of the Bank Street / City Lore Center for Folk Arts in Education (New York, US); the staff of the National Museum of the American Indian; Eric Maddern (Gwynedd, Wales); Elspeth Robb (New South Wales, Australia); Cathy Fischgrund (London, England); Ang Grunsel (Oxfam Library, London, England); Harold Underdown (New York, US); Yaa Connelly (Ghana); Harry Ioannides (Limassol, Cyprus); Sergey Karmamny (Moscow, Russia); Mahmoud Mirfatali (Iran); Sonia Bennister (Huddersfield, England); Caroline Cousins (Jamaica); Suzel Cresson (Le Touquet, France); Carolyn Evans (Wales); Nada Svilar (former Yugoslavia); Tom Macmillan, Linden Lodge, Wimbledon (London, England); Cynthia Casey (Hong Kong); Irving Callander (Trinidad), and everyone who helped to make this book possible.

ISLINGTON

Floella Benj

producer

to makin

She has writ

of her o

She is in

Her l

Sheila Mox

School of A

and has

Her insp

travels all

Stone Girl

by Saviou

SKIP ACROSS THE OCEAN

Nursery rhymes from
around the world
collected by

FLOELLA BENJAMIN

Illustrated by

SHEILA MOXLEY

F

FRANCES LINCOLN
CHILDREN'S BOOKS

CONTENTS

★ LULLABIES ★

ACTION ✋ RHYMES

✽ NATURE ✽

LUCKY ♥ DIP

The world has a treasure chest of lullabies and nursery rhymes which is opened every time a child is born. I can still hear my mother's voice singing lullabies to me and when I became a mother, I sang them to my children. It gave us a lovely feeling of togetherness. Though my children are older now, their favourite childhood rhymes still comfort them whenever they feel unhappy.

★

Working with children has made me realise that nursery rhymes are precious and should be shared by everyone and preserved for always. Rhymes are children's first introduction to rhythm, poetry, music and the world around them, often nurturing their instinctive awareness of nature. They explore feelings and help children to develop important social skills while passing on cultural values and traditions to the next generation. That's why I decided to put together a collection of traditional rhymes from all over the world.

★

As the rhymes flooded in from relatives and friends spread across the world, I was amazed at the similarities between them. Many carry the same emotions and messages while still reflecting the different countries and cultures in which they are set. Some of the rhymes are shown in their original language as well as English.

★

It is difficult to know where all the rhymes originated because many have travelled across oceans and continents. Different cultures have adopted the rhymes and passed them on to *their* children. One that I loved singing as a little girl is '*I am a Little Dutch Girl*' - a rhyme in English about a Dutch girl, which my mother sang to me in Trinidad and I, in turn, sang it to my children in London! No doubt, this rhyme with others, will be passed on to generations to come, all over the world.

Floella Benjamin

LIZZIE

Lizzie Lizzie, spinning top,
Ever dancing, never stop.
Dancing in the morning dew,
Barefoot tap, one two, one two.

Lizzie Lizzie, spinning top,
Ever dancing, never stop.
Dancing in the sun's warm rays,
Shining brightly at midday.

Lizzie Lizzie, spinning top,

Ever dancing, never stop.

Dancing as the sun sinks low,

Setting all the lake aglow.

Now she's lying in her bed,

Rosy pillow 'neath her head.

Round the fence a dream comes creeping,

Softly now ... for Lizzie's sleeping.

POLAND

9

WAMPANOAG LULLABY

Wunny Wunny Krietta

Tashinahanu

Wunny Wamiaquene

Wunnitu Tahnam

Beautiful Beautiful Bundle

The Wind laughs

All is Peace and Beauty

Beautiful Heart-finder

Wampanoag peoples, South-east New England, NORTH AMERICA

SCHLAF, KINDLEIN, SCHLAF

Schlaf, Kindlein, schlaf,

Dein Vater hütet die Schaf,

Deine Mutter schüttelt's Bäumelein,

Und leise fällt ein Träumelein,

Schlaf, Kindlein, schlaf.

★

Sleep, baby, sleep,

Thy father tends the sheep,

Thy mother rocks the slumber tree,

And softly falls a dream for thee.

Sleep, baby, sleep.

GERMANY

11

LULLABY

Lullaby my baby, lullaby my darling,

Lullaby my baby, lullaby my darling.

There above us, baby, we can see the sky.

There away beyond us

Is the sunlight in the garden.

★

Lullaby my baby, lullaby my darling,

Lullaby my baby, lullaby my darling.

Where, my little one, has your mother gone?

She's gone to the pond where blue lilies grow.

★

Lullaby my baby, lullaby my darling,

Lullaby my baby, lullaby my darling.

When at night, my son,

Clouds come over the moon

Then it's time, my son,

To sleep and cease to cry.

SRI LANKA

EL COQUÍ

El Coquí sings a sweet song at twilight.

He is singing as sleep comes to me.

When I wake alone in the moonlight

El Coquí sings goodnight from the tree.

Coquí, coquí, coquí, quí, quí, quí,

Coquí, coquí, coquí, coquí, quí, quí, quí.

PUERTO RICO

El Coquí is Spanish for 'Tree Toad'

13

14

CRADLESONG OF
THE SPARROWS

Little chick, chick, hey-ah!

Little chick, chick, hey-ah!

Little palm seed,

From dusk to dawn

I'll swing you back and forth,

I'll swing you back and forth.

Aguaruna tribe, PERU

COMFORTING SONG

Do not cry, little one,

Your father will fetch you.

He is coming

As soon as he has made

His new harpoon head.

Do not cry, little one.

Do not weep.

Inuit peoples, GREENLAND/ARCTIC CANADA

HUSH'N BYE

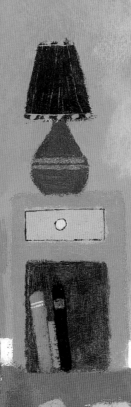

Hush'n bye, don't you cry,

Oh, you pretty little baby,

When you wake you'll have sweet cake,

And all the pretty little ponies.

A brown and a grey, and a black and a bay,

And all the pretty little ponies.

Appalachian and Southern States, NORTH AMERICA

17

ACTION RHYMES

ÈKIN, ÈKEJI, ÈKETA

Èkin ni ebi pa mi,

Èkeji ni iya ọsi ńilè,

Èketa ni jè ka ji nka loko,

Èkeri ni bi oloko ba mu è?

Èkarùn ni ma wò ibòmi.

The first one says, I'm hungry,

The second says, mother is not home,

The third one says, let's get something at the farm,

The fourth one says, what if the farmer catches us?

The fifth one says, I'll look the other way.

Yoruba tribe, NIGERIA

This rhyme is also well known among the *Fanti* of Ghana.
✋ While reciting the rhyme, stretch out the baby's hands, touching
and folding each finger in turn and sticking the thumb out at the end.

19

CANOE SONG

My paddle's keen and bright,

Flashing with silver.

Follow the wild goose flight,

Dip, dip and swing.

Dip, dip and swing her back,

Flashing silver.

Swift as the wild goose flies,

Dip, dip and swing.

CANADA

Sit on the floor, rest your child between your knees facing you. Hold her hands and rock backwards and forwards to mimic the movement of the boat.

ЗАЙКА БЕЛЕНЬКИЙ СИДИТ
LITTLE WHITE RABBIT

Зайка беленький сидит,
Он ушами шевелит,
Вот так, вот так
Он ушами шевелит.

Little white rabbit sits,

He wiggles his ears -

This way and that,

He wiggles his ears.

Little rabbit is cold,

He must warm his paws -

Clap, clap, clap, clap,

He must warm his paws.

Someone frightened little rabbit,

He jumped up... and ran away.

RUSSIA

Echo the rabbit's actions with your baby -
wiggle his ears, clap his hands, then lift him
high in the air.

21

COME HARVEST

Come now, the ripe flax
We're harvesting today.
Card, card it well and spin, spin away.
Soon we will weave
Our clothes bright and gay,
Then off we go a-dancing.

Donk, donk, donk. Donk, donk, donk.
Spools whirl around, spools whirl around.
Donk, donk, donk. Donk, donk, donk.
Off we go a-dancing.

Come now, the flax
We're carding today.
Card, card it well and spin, spin away.
Soon we will weave
Our clothes bright and gay,
Then off we go a-dancing.

Come now, the finest cloth
We're weaving today.
Spinning is done, we weave, weave away.
Soon we will weave
Our clothes bright and gay,
Then off we go a-dancing.

SWEDEN

✋ Echo the whirling spools by bouncing and twisting
your baby on your knee.

23

CLAP HANDS

Clap hands for Mammy,
Till Daddy come,
Bring cake and sugar plum,
And give baby some.
When Daddy come he will kiss and say boo,
This is to show Daddy's love is true.

TRINIDAD

CLAP HANDIES

Clap handies, clap handies,
Till Daddy comes home,
Chocolate in his pocket,
For Nuala* alone.

IRELAND
* Put in your baby's name.

GEE UP A CHAPAILLÍN

"How many miles from this to Dublin?"

"Threescore and ten, Sir."

"Will I be back there by candlelight?"

"Yes, and back again, Sir."

"Gee up a chapaillín,
Gee up a chapaillín,
Gee up a chapaillín,
A chapaillín again, Sir!"

IRELAND

* *Capaillín* is Irish for little horse.
* Bounce your baby slowly for the first verse,
then faster and faster as you 'gee up'.

THE SINGING BIRD

I saw a redbird in the air,
A redbird in a tree,
But a redbird in a bramble bush
Was the one that sang to me.

Birdie, birdie in the air,
Birdie in the tree!
But the birdie I like best of all
Is the one that sings to me!

I saw a blackbird in the air,
A blackbird in a tree,
But a blackbird in a bramble bush
Was the one that sang to me.

I saw a bluebird in the air,
A bluebird in a tree,
But a bluebird in a bramble bush
Was the one that sang to me.

Tennessee, NORTH AMERICA

27

LIULI,
LIULI, LIULI

Liuli, liuli, liuli,

In the pigeons flew,

They sat on the bed,

And they began to coo,

Quietly putting the child to sleep.

"Sleep, little one, sleep,

Do not open your eyes!"

RUSSIA

屋根の上の鯉のぼり
ABOVE THE ROOFTOPS

屋根より高い鯉のぼり
大きな真鯉はお父さん
小さい緋鯉は子供たち
面白そうに泳いでる。
*
High above the rooftop,

See carp streamers fly.

See the big black carp up there,

That one is the father.

See the small golden carp,

They are the children.

See them gaily swimming by,

Gaily swimming by.

JAPAN

29

LITTLE ELEPHANT
SWAYING

Little elephant swaying,

Growing up breathing fresh air

And eating fresh branches.

Little elephant,

Swaying this way and that,

Eating the heart of the kia plant.

Hindi-speaking peoples, INDIA

KALEEBA!

Ssemusajja agenda, kaleeba!*

Onnambira abali ek'eyo, kaleeba!

Ebinyonyi biri ku luzzi, kaleeba!

Byambadde ensimbi, kaleeba!

Nsimbi n'obutiiti, kaleeba!

A...a...kyo ki? Kaleeba!

Kyuka n'ondeeba! Kaleeba!

✱

Little one passing by, look!

Take a message for me, look!

You just say a bird is here at the well,

And he's wearing cowrie shells, look!

He's got cowries and many fine beads!

Turn back look at me? Look!

Turn back and look at me! Look!

UGANDA

* *Kaleeba* is an old Luganda word for 'Look'.

LULLABY
OF A DOG
TO HER PUP

Here,

You like to be nursed

In your young years

You floppy thing.

Here,

You like to be nursed,

Little tail,

You wobbly one.

Crow Indians, Northern Plains, NORTH AMERICA

छोटी सी चिड़िया
LITTLE BIRD

चिड़िया आती है,
दाना चुगती है,
थोड़ा सा पानी पी के,
दूर उड़ जाती है!

*

Bird comes,

Eats some seed,

Drinks a little water

And flies away!

Hindi-speaking peoples, INDIA

KELLA BUKK

Kella Bukk, Kella Blakk,
Kella liten Nevetapp!
Rosa, Dokka, Nykla, Sokka,
Storspenna, Spelemann!
Burt i Fljellom!

*

Nanny goat, Billy goat,
Little kid with fluffy coat!
Rosie, Dolly, Peggy, Molly,
Old long-legs Frisky,
Bonny May!
And Player on the mountain!

NORWAY

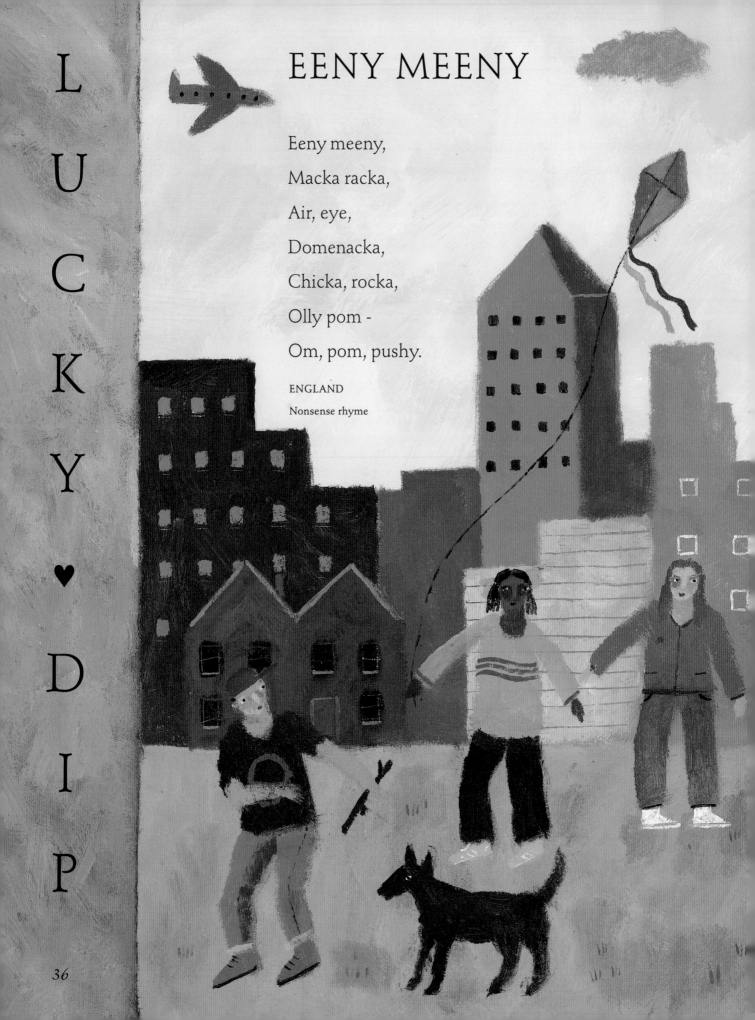

EENY MEENY

Eeny meeny,

Macka racka,

Air, eye,

Domenacka,

Chicka, rocka,

Olly pom -

Om, pom, pushy.

ENGLAND
Nonsense rhyme

KYE KYE KULE

Kye Kye Kule

Kye Kye Kofi Sa

Kofi Salanga

Katakyi Langa

Lalasu Lala

Kum adende

Kokrokoo ekor

Kokrokoo ebien

Kokrokoo ebiasa

Kokrokoo anan

Kokrokoo enum

Akaa yie.

Fanti tribe, GHANA
Action rhyme using nonsense words

CHILDREN, CHILDREN

Children, children.

Yes, Mama?

Where did you went to?

To see Granpa.

What did he give you?

Bread and patata.

Where did you put it?

Upon de ledge.

Suppose it drop.

I don't give a rap.

ANTIGUA

AL CORRO DE LA PATATA

Al corro de la patata,

Comeremos ensalada,

Como comen los señores,

Naranjitas y limones,

A lupe! A lupe!

Sentadita me quedé.

♥

In a circle of potatoes,

We will eat salad,

While the masters eat

Small oranges and lemons,

Hurray! Hurray!

I stayed sitting down.

SPAIN

This is similar to the English rhyme
Ring O'Roses.

KOOKABURRA

Kookaburra sits on the old gum tree,

Merry, merry king of the Bush is he.

Laugh, kookaburra,

Laugh, kookaburra,

Gay your life must be.

AUSTRALIA

拉大鋸
PULLING THE SAW

拉大鋸，
扯大鋸，
楊大頭蓋房子，
給貝貝取娘子。

Push the saw,

Pull the saw,

Big Head Yang

Builds a house,

So his child

Can find a spouse.

CHINA

FRÈRE JACQUES

Frère Jacques, Frère Jacques,
Dormez-vous, dormez-vous?
Sonnez les mâtines,
Sonnez les mâtines,
Ding, dang, dong.
Ding, dang, dong.

♥

Are you sleeping, are you sleeping,
Brother John, Brother John?
Morning bells are ringing,
Morning bells are ringing,
Ding, dang, dong.
Ding, dang, dong.

FRANCE

RIDE A
COCK HORSE

Ride a cock horse
To Banbury Cross,
To see a fine lady
Upon a white horse.
With rings on her fingers
And bells on her toes,
She shall have music
Wherever she goes.

ENGLAND

MANGOES

Mangoes, mangoes, mangoes.

Mango rose, mango starch, mango starch.

Ah wan' a penny to buy mango rose, mango starch.

Gimme penny to buy mango rose, mango starch.

Mango zabico, calabash,

Savez-vous, all for me,

Mango zabico, calabash,

Savez-vous, all for me.

Mangoes, mangoes, mangoes.

TRINIDAD

BROWN GIRL IN THE RING

There's a brown girl in the ring,

Tra la la la la,

There's a brown girl in the ring,

Tra la la la la,

There's a brown girl in the ring,

Tra la la la la,

For she like sugar and I like plum.

Then you skip across the ocean,

Tra la la la la,

Then you skip across the ocean,

Tra la la la la,

Then you skip across the ocean,

Tra la la la la,

For she like sugar and I like plum.

TRINIDAD

MORE TITLES FROM
FRANCES LINCOLN CHILDREN'S BOOKS

My Two Grannies
Floella Benjamin
Illustrated by Margaret Chamberlain

"A lovely story book with wonderful illustrations and
multicultural experiences and traditions."
Nursery Education Plus

Acker Backa Boo!
Opal Dunn
Illustrated by Susan Winter

Fantastic playground action rhymes
from all over the world.

W is for World
A Round-the-World ABC
Kate Cave
In association with Oxfam

Invites children to focus on the similarities
as well as the differences of other cultures.

Frances Lincoln titles are available from all good bookshops.
You can also buy books and find out more about your favourite titles,
authors and illustrators on our website: www.franceslincoln.com